HELEN HIG

Helen Highwater is the amazing story of the greatest heroine the town of Chucklewick has ever known, who swims over six hundred miles in a record-breaking attempt to raise a million pounds. If she fails, Major Leech and the evil BUMM (British Urban Mis-Management) will pull down her parents' chip-shop and the high street; if she succeeds, it will be a haze of film crews, limousines and banquets and Chucklewick will be saved for ever.

Join Helen on her amazing journey from Land's End to John o'Groat's in a fast-paced narrative poem by one of today's most popular poets.

Roger McGough was born in Liverpool and in the late sixties and early seventies he was a member of the group The Scaffold. He is best known as a writer of plays and poems for both adults and children, and he spends much of his time performing his work on tour. He now lives in London.

HELEN HIGHWATER

A Shropshire Lass

Roger McGough

Illustrated by Martin Chatterton

PUFFIN BOOKS

For Ming and Maddy

PUFFIN BOOKS

Published by the Penguin Group
Penguin Books Ltd, 27 Wrights Lane, London W8 5TZ, England
Viking Penguin, a division of Penguin Books USA Inc.
375 Hudson Street, New York, New York 10014, USA
Penguin Books Australia Ltd, Ringwood, Victoria, Australia
Penguin Books Canada Ltd, 2801 John Street, Markham, Ontario, Canada L3R 1B4
Penguin Books (NZ) Ltd, 182–190 Wairau Road, Auckland 10, New Zealand

Penguin Books Ltd, Registered Offices: Harmondsworth, Middlesex, England

First published by Viking Kestrel 1989
Published in Puffin Books 1991
1 3 5 7 9 10 8 6 4 2

Text copyright © Roger McGough, 1989
Illustrations copyright © Martin Chatterton, 1989
All rights reserved

Printed in England by Clays Ltd, St Ives plc
Filmset in Linotron Palatino

Outside a chip-shop in Shropshire
   (Yes, I know that's hard to say)
A foundling was discovered
   One cold November day.

Abandoned by its mother
   (Was she heartless? Maybe)
But fortune was to smile
   Upon that tiny baby.

For Mr and Mrs Highwater
  (To friends, Nigel and Joan)
Decided that night to care for the mite
  And bring it up as their own.

Caroline? Debbie? Fiona?
  Sharon? Nicola? Paula?
They went through hell and high water
  Wondering what to call her.

And so she was christened Helen
  (The name fitted like a glove)
And they brought her up in an atmosphere
  Of beef dripping and love.

Weaned from the start on chip-butties
  Washed down with cod-liver oil
She blossomed and bloomed, one could
    only assume
  Such a diet was fit for a Royal.

A nice piece of plaice for breakfast
    Haddock and chips for tea
Lunch on the run, fried cod in a bun
    She grew up tall as a tree.

Strong as oxen was Helen
    With super recuperative powers
She could run at a gallop all over Salop
    Then do squats and press-ups for hours.

The lass could swim like an angel
    (One wearing snorkel and flippers)
Two hundred breadths without breathing
    Then home to a panful of kippers.

Was it the fish that did it?
Or the vinegar trickling through?
Or maybe the batter? It doesn't matter,
Whatever it was, she G-R-E-W.

Meanwhile, elsewhere in the story
    (in the Town Hall, to be precise)
Albert Leech was up to something
    And that something wasn't nice.

Nor was he, and he was the Mayor
    (Whenever you see him hiss)
As I say, he was up to something
    And the something up was this . . .

Albert too owned a chippy
    In Crematorium Square
Between the gasworks and the tannery
    And it smelled like a durianimal's* lair.

Kids called him 'Spit-in-the-boiler'
    For his chips were soggy with fat
And his fish just skin with bones chucked in
    You wouldn't feed them to a cat.

He even charged for salt and vinegar
    (Imagine anyone so mean)
Then he'd try and diddle you with the change
    And his pickled eggs were obscene.

Durianimal: A strange creature found in Malaya. Half animal, half
fruit, it has an offensive smell but a pleasant taste.

A widower, he lived with his daughter
   Whom he treated like a slave
Edna, who was never seen to smile
   And silent she was, as the grave.

And oh, how he hated the Highwaters
   Until one evening he swore
By Neptune, the fishfrier's god
   To cry, 'Haddock!' and let slip the dogs
    of war.

*

British Urban Mis-Management
   (Known the world over as BUMM)
Had plush offices in Mayfair
   And there Mayor Leech had come.

To explain his scheme to the governors
   Who agreed to do their best
To dump a town centre in Chucklewick
   Identikit, just like the rest.

Back in Town Hall he made long speeches
  With quotations in Latin and Greek
Until councillors, bored, dozed off and snored
  Then he pushed through his plan (The Sneak).

The plan was to pull down the High Street
  (Where Highwaters' proudly held sway)
To build an arcade and a car-park
  In concrete all gloomy and grey.

Nigel had not an inkling
  Of the misfortune lying in store
New potatoes he was crinkling
  When suddenly through the door . . .

Two thugs from BUMM came charging
  Barged to the head of the queue
And served him a chit, on which was writ:
  'Dear sir, it's curtains for you.'

The bad news spread like wildfire
  And them that were due for the chop
Called an emergency meeting
  That night above Highwaters' shop.

Albert Leech turned up to gloat
  With his pathetic next of kin
But Helen barred them at the door
  And refused to let them in.

'You've had your chips,' he sneered,
  'BUMM now holds the lease
Unless you can find a million pounds
  Right quick, they call the police.'

A million pounds? A £1,000,000?
  How can we raise a million pounds?
A £1,000,000? A million pounds?
  No one can raise a £1,000,000.

'I've got an idea,' shouted Helen.
  Joan shushed them, 'Let the girl speak.'
'From Land's End to John o'Groat's,
  I can do it in under a week.'

Everyone smiled and nodded politely.
   'Nice try, lass, it's already been run,
Walked, jogged, skipped and bi-cycled,
   You name it, we're afraid it's been done.'

'Not swum, though,' cried Helen steadfastly.
   'Swum?' they said. 'Swum as in swim?'
They looked at each other and nodded
   (Nice girl, young Helen, but dim).

But dim she was not, and soon they forgot
　　Their doubts, as she expanded
On her plan to swim six hundred miles
　　Overland and single-handed.

And when she'd done with expanding
　　It was so quiet you could hear a gum drop
Then everyone cheered like crazy
　　'Land's End,' they cried, 'next stop.'

'But first let's raise the sponsorship
　　Through radio, press and TV.'
Flora Bundle raised a manicured hand,
　　'You can leave that side to me.

A friend of a friend of my brother-in-law
　　Knows a cousin of Elton John
And once I had a record request
　　Nearly played on Radio One.'

There remained only the minor details
　　Like the truck and the polythene pool
But she left all that to the grown-ups
　　It was bed-time, and tomorrow was school.

Albert Leech switched off the telly
  His face all snarly and sour
With a newsflash of Helen's progress
  Being transmitted every hour.

How she'd swum across Bodmin and Dartmoor
  In a swimming-pool on wheels
Then crossed the Bristol Channel
  In the company of seals.

And straight up the River Severn
  With a deceptively easy crawl
Reaching Birmingham via Worcester
  In next to no time at all.

'Do cheer up, father,' said Edna,
   'I'll bring you some cocoa in bed,
For you've got to admit she's fantastically fit.'
   'Oh shut up, you twit,' he said.

'I may seem mean and I may seem cruel
   But I'm doing it for the best
Until Helen is driven out of our lives
   I swear I'll never rest.'

Then he slammed the door behind him
   And clattered into the night.
Then alone in the room's chill darkness
   Edna saw just a glimmer of light.

The crowds in Gas Street Basin
    Had gathered since break of day
To catch a glimpse of their heroine
    As she butterflew on her way.

Like a dolphin she rose from the water
    To acknowledge the deafening applause
Then amateur divers collected the fivers
    Thrown in, in support of the cause.

Up the Shropshire Union Canal
  Into the River Weaver at Crewe
Where she changed into a new bathing
    costume
  (Because everyone changes at Crewe).

When she swam the River Mersey
  Half of Liverpool turned up
You could forgive a stranger thinking
  That both teams had won the Cup.

Then straight up north on the motorway
With Nigel at the wheel
Keeping her steady at seventy
To maintain an even keel.

At midnight, Nigel pulled over
    And watched by quizzical sheep
Helped Helen out of the water
    For soup and a snippet of sleep.

In the convoy was a caravan
    Nothing fancy, but Helen adored
To sleep like a monk on the plywood bunk
    (Though the bath she largely ignored).

Then up with the lark and the kestrel
    Forgetting the pains and the aches
For today was a day she'd remember
    The day she swam through the lakes.

Ullswater

Rydal Water

Derwent Water

Hawes Water

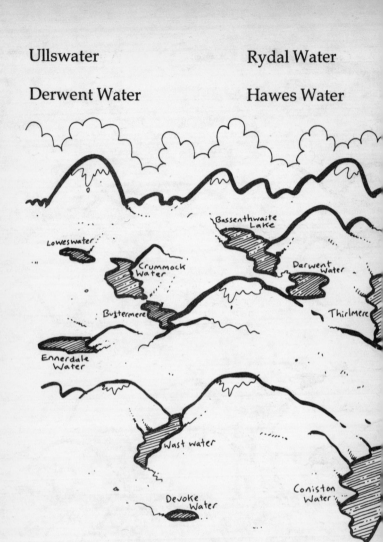

Her swimming matched the beauty of each lake.

Grasmere   Windermere

Buttermere   Thirlmere

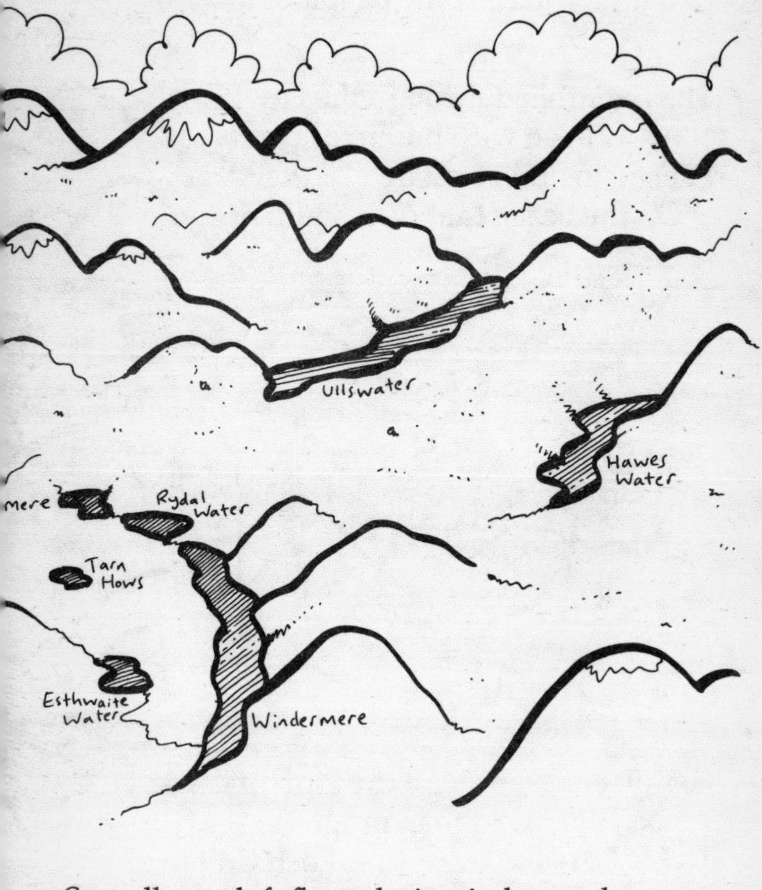

Ullswater

Hawes Water

mere

Rydal Water

Tarn Hows

Esthwaite Water

Windermere

Speedboats left floundering in her wake.

Then a leisurely swim up the Eden
    Where Hadrian's Wall stands proud
And into the Nith at Dumfries
    With the skirl of the bagpipes loud.

The river rolled through the Lowlands
    And Helen with hours to spare
Paused to build a castle
    On the beach that runs south of Ayr.

Her plan was to swim the Firth of Clyde
    Loch Fyne and then progress
To Loch Awe, Loch Etive, Loch Creran
    Loch Linnhe, Loch Lochy, Loch Ness.

'That's it,' cried Albert (gone purple)
    Pointing to the Chucklewick Express,
'That's where she'll get her come-uppance,
    She'll go to her doom in Loch Ness!'

He said no more that evening
    But disappeared into his shed
And the banging and the clanging
    Kept Edna awake in her bed.

He was still hard at it next morning
    When she opened the workshop door
And the tea and the pikelets went crashing
    At the sight of the sight that she saw.

✽

THE JUGGERNAUT'S SONG

I'm a wart
Spoil-sport
I'm a juggernaut.

I'm a Rocker
Right shocker
Real nasty sort.

My hair is slicked with grease
   And I wear dark shades
Gimme shoes instead of wheels
   And they'd be blue suedes.

I'm a mean-minded bully
   Who can't take a joke
I smoke a filthy pipe
   And I blow black smoke.

I'm a slug, ugh, ugh
I'm a juggernaut
Big bug, chug chug
I'm a juggernaut.

When I take the motorway
    Better step aside
A cop tried to stop me once
    That copper died.

Articulated mayhem
   Poison in my wake
Hear the mother scream
   As I hit the brake.

I'm a slug, ugh, ugh
I'm a juggernaut
Big bug, chug chug
I'm a juggernaut.

Forty tons of muscle
  Lunatic on wheels
Knowing the excitement
  A gangster feels.

Chasing little rabbits
  Putting birds to flight
Shaking leaves from the trees
  Just for spite.

I'm a slug, ugh, ugh
I'm a juggernaut
Big bug, chug chug
I'm a juggernaut.

Devil hell-for-leather
  Beelzebub express
Cargo of mischief
  Bound for . . . Loch Ness.

Albert got to Loch Ness on the Thursday
  (The day before Helen was due)
And tested his evil contraption
  In a bay that was hidden from view.

Edna, poor thing, could not comprehend
  What the motorized monster was for
Or why her father wore a frogman's suit
  And wielded a hungry chainsaw.

'Oh father, I cannot comprehend
  What the motorized monster is for
Or why you are wearing a frogman's suit
  And wielding a hungry chainsaw.'

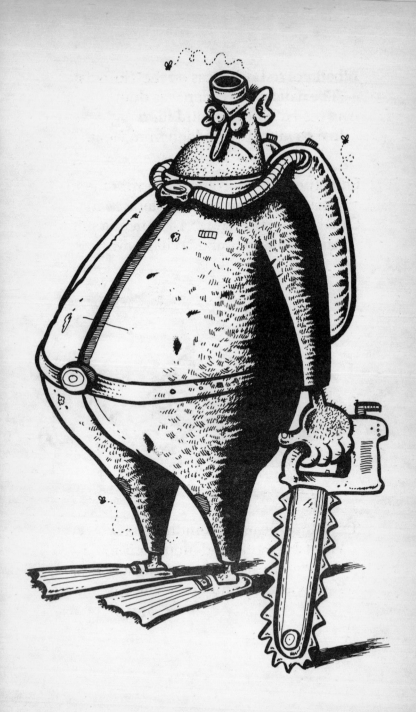

Whatever it was he was doing
   Albert didn't any more
Because he'd never heard his daughter
   Use so many words before.

Only then (too late) he realized
   That they'd slowly grown apart
So he took off his snorkel and goggles
   And (too late) poured out his heart:

'In your teens remember the baby you bore?
   Stillborn, I said, how you cried.
A child yourself, you could never have coped.
   Well, Edna, I confess that I lied.

Ashamed for you, I took it that night
  To drown like an unloved pup
When suddenly, out of the river
  A serpent-like monster reared up.

The thing roared and I panicked
I turned and ran into town
And upon the nearest doorstep
I lay your daughter down.

Helen is proof of that terrible sin
    And the guilt has caused endless pain
The secret dies only when she does
    Only then I'll be happy again.'

Then he climbed inside his monster
    Leaving Edna dumb with shock
And switching on the engine
    Sailed away into the loch.

In the Fisherman's Arms a fisherman
   Sipping Scotch to keep out the cold
Tells a story (though no one believes him)
   And this is the story he told:

'Och, I was oot there takin' it easy
  Without a care in the world
When I came over kind of queasy
  As the water aroond me swirled.

An' then a whoppin' great beastie
Hove to on the starboard bow
Makin' a sort of whirrin' sound
(In nightmares, I still hear it now).

It had eyes like motor-car headlamps
  And teeth that buzzed like a saw
I took a wee dram to keep out the cramps
  Then dropped to my knees on the floor.

Holy sporran, then behind it
  A second monster reared on high
Serpent-like yet familiar
  Nessie's shadow filled the sky!

Wi' a roar that echoed through the glen
  She fell upon her foe
Wrapped herself aroond it then
  And dragged it doon below.

Bubbles, aye, and nothing else
  Save silence, harsh as a scream.
Now my hair is white, for I aged overnight
  Dinnae tell me 'twas all but a dream.'

Helen, happily unaware
  Of the battle of the giants
And needing some tuition
  In geography and science,

Was given extra-mural lessons
  On her way to Inverness
By an Olympic synchronized swimmer
  With a Ph.D. no less.

They twirled and turned in unison
  Young bodies slim and sleek
A pair of Siamese porpoise-twins
  Would have envied their technique.

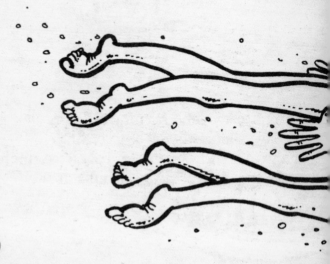

At Inverness they parted
   (Ph.D. had a boyfriend in Perth)
While Helen, feeling tired now,
   Struck out into the Moray Firth.

But the North Sea was rough and unfriendly
   And Helen began to feel sick
So at Joan's request decided to rest
   And swam up the coast road to Wick.

Whereupon the weather cleared
   And the water was smooth as an egg
As Helen went down to the sea again
   For the last triumphant leg.

John o'Groat's (not quite Acapulco)
Had never witnessed such a day
As Helen rounded Duncansby Head
And crawled ashore in the Bay.

The press were there in their hundreds
  And Caithness turned out in force
To see if the cheque for a million pounds
  Could be claimed. And could it? Of course.

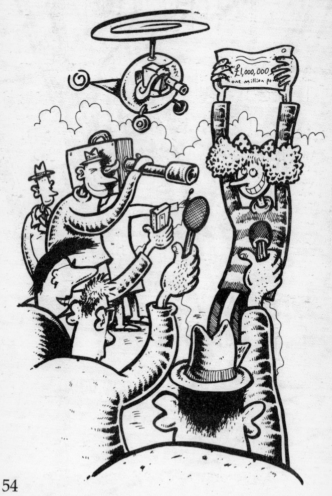

The following week for Helen
  Remains a glamorous haze
As limousines and banquets
  And film-crews filled her days.

But she was glad when it was over
  (Would those flash-bulbs ever stop?)
Back to the cosy reality
  Of school and the friendly shop.

Albert Leech's disappearance
  Disappeared in all the fuss
Until Joan, out shopping one afternoon,
  Met Edna on a 48 bus.

No one knows what they talked about
  But at midnight, it appears
That the bus ended back at the terminus
  With the two of them in tears.

✱

So whenever you're popping through
   Shropshire
 (Yes, I know that's hard to say)
Do yourself a favour
  Stop at Chucklewick on the way.

Head straight for Highwaters' Restaurant
  And say when you see Joan and Nige,
'An autographed picture of Helen, please.'
  They'll be only too glad to oblige.

And don't be surprised to see Edna
  Who they took in to work alongside
She's still not one for rabbiting on
  But now there's a smile a mile wide.

And Helen? Well she may pop in
  But she's training hard each day
For the 'Save the Loch Ness Monster' fund
  (She's going to water-ski to Bombay!)